Bats in Trouble

Pamela McDowell
illustrated by Kasia Charko

ORCA BOOK PUBLISHERS

Library and Archives Canada Cataloguing in Publication

Bats in trouble / Pamela McDowell ; illustrated by Kasia Charko.
(Orca echoes)

Issued in print and electronic formats.
ISBN 978-1-4598-1403-5 (softcover).—ISBN 978-1-4598-1404-2 (pdf).—
ISBN 978-1-4598-1405-9 (epub)

I. Charko, Kasia, 1949-, illustrator II. Title. III. Series: Orca echoes
PS8625.D785B38 2017 jC813'.6 C2017-900842-0
C2017-900843-9

First published in the United States, 2017
Library of Congress Control Number: 2017933012

Summary: In this early chapter book, Cricket and her friends rally the town of Pincher Creek to save migrating bats being killed by newly installed wind turbines.

Orca Book Publishers gratefully acknowledges the support for its publishing programs provided by the following agencies: the Government of Canada through the Canada Book Fund and the Canada Council for the Arts, and the Province of British Columbia through the BC Arts Council and the Book Publishing Tax Credit.

Edited by Liz Kemp
Cover artwork and interior illustrations by Kasia Charko
Author photo by Ellen Gasser

ORCA BOOK PUBLISHERS
www.orcabook.com

Printed and bound in Canada.

20 19 18 17 • 4 3 2 1

For Tessa, who is always
up for adventure.

Chapter One

"The second time Angelica went up the stairs, she heard the music again. She crept slowly, stepping over the hole in the fourth stair. Her heart pounded. *Fa-thump, fa-thump, fa-thump*." Tyler paused and leaned forward to poke the logs in the fire pit.

"Don't stop now," Shilo said. She squished closer to Cricket and grabbed her hand. "Did she see the ghost? Was it there?"

Tyler nodded, his face serious. "Angelica held her breath and listened. *Creak-creak. Creak-creak*. It repeated over and over. *Creak-creak. Creak-creak*. She tiptoed down the hall, following the beam of her flashlight. Spiders scurried out of her way."

"Ouch, don't squeeze so tight!" Cricket said.

"Sorry. He said there were spiders."

"It was colder at the end of the hall. The creaking got louder. Suddenly Angelica's flashlight flickered and went out. She froze. The hall was completely dark. She would never find her way back down the stairs. She had to go forward."

Crack! A log in the fire popped and sent a shower of sparks up in the air. The girls jumped. Shilo gasped.

"*Creak-creak. Creak-creak.* The sound was coming from the room at the end of the hall. Light began to glow from a crack under the door. The air in the hallway was cold. Angelica took a deep breath and peeked through the door. But she leaned in too far—the door swung wide open and she fell into the room!"

Crack! Another log popped. Something dark flew over the girls' heads.

Cricket ducked. "What was that?"

Small dark bodies zoomed past.

Shilo screamed. "Bats!"

Cricket's grandpa stepped out onto the farmhouse porch. "Everything all right down there, Tyler? Cricket?"

Tyler was laughing. "Yes, Grandpa. I just scared the girls with a ghost story, that's all."

"No you didn't! Something flew at us. That's what made us scream." Cricket narrowed her eyes. "Did you throw something at us, Tyler? To scare us?" She knew her older brother liked to play pranks. But Tyler laughed and shook his head.

"Those were bats, Cricket. I'm sure of it," Shilo said. She still had her arms over her head as she crouched down low.

"Could be. We see lots of bats out here this time of year," Cricket's grandpa, Mr. McKay, said. "They keep the bugs from destroying our crops, so we're happy to see them."

Cricket and Tyler's grandparents lived on a large farm near Pincher Creek.

The wide, rolling hills were very different from the rocky forest where Cricket and Tyler lived, in Waterton Lakes National Park. Every summer, the kids visited the farm for a few weeks, and this year Shilo, Cricket's best friend, had joined them. They were all looking forward to participating in the Pincher Creek parade with Grandpa McKay.

Shilo groaned. "You didn't warn me about the bats, Cricket!"

"I didn't know about—" Cricket started to say, but it was too late. Shilo was running full speed to the porch.

Chapter Two

"What are you girls up to today?" Grandpa McKay poured himself a cup of coffee and sat down at the kitchen table.

"We thought we'd go for a walk," Cricket said. She finished her last bite of toast. "Maybe out toward the back pasture this time."

Grandpa nodded. "Do you need a pail for crickets?" He winked at Shilo.

Cricket rolled her eyes. "No, Grandpa. We don't do that anymore." Back when she was five, she had collected hundreds of crickets, hoping to start a cricket zoo. She let them go eventually, but by then Grandpa had started calling her Cricket. The nickname stuck.

"Will you be back for lunch?" Grandma McKay asked.

Cricket nodded. "Yup. You ready, Shilo?"

"Yup." Shilo grabbed her red ballcap. "Thanks for breakfast, Mrs. McKay."

The girls stepped outside, and Cooper, an old border collie, jumped up from his snooze. His ears perked up and his tail wagged hopefully. When Cricket nodded to him, he yipped and spun in circles. Cooper was so smart, Cricket's grandpa used hand signals and whistles

to tell him to bring in the cows. As the girls walked through the pasture, Cooper raced ahead, zigzagging back and forth.

"What's he looking for?" Shilo asked.

"Ground squirrels, probably. He likes to chase them, but he's never caught one."

The girls were being watched as they walked through the crunchy brown grass. Little brown heads popped up from burrows. Brave ground squirrels stood up on their hind legs and squeaked at the girls. They scurried back down their burrows when they saw Cooper coming.

"Wow, I didn't know your grandpa had one of those huge windmills!"

Up on the ridge in front of them stood five white wind turbines. One was inside the pasture. The arms spun slowly, even though Cricket couldn't feel a breeze.

"I didn't know either. It reminds me of an airplane—you know, one of those giant white ones."

As the girls got closer, they could feel vibrations through the ground.

"Do you hear that hum?"

"Barely," Shilo said. "What's wrong with Cooper?"

The dog was sitting motionless, staring at the turbine. He watched the girls continue closer but refused to move.

"That's weird." Cricket held up her palm, and Cooper lay down. "I guess he doesn't like the vibrations or something."

As the girls got closer to the turbine, they saw the ends of the blades were moving much faster than they had first appeared to be. The base of the turbine

was huge. If the girls held hands with five friends, they still wouldn't stretch all the way around it.

"Ew! Look, Cricket." Shilo pointed to something in the grass near her foot. "Is it a mouse?"

Cricket crouched down to have a closer look. The furry brown body was smaller than her fist. It looked a bit like a mouse, but it had small ears, and its front legs were different.

"I think it's a bat. See that dark skin there? I think that's its wing."

"Ah! Don't touch it! You can get rabies from bats."

"Poor little guy. I wonder what killed it." Cricket looked up at the turbine blades cutting through the air above her head. "Do you think he ran into the turbine last night?"

"It does look pretty deadly, but don't bats have super good vision in the dark?" Shilo walked around the turbine, keeping her eyes on the ground. "Here's another one!"

The second bat was a bit smaller. It was on its back, and its wings were spread out.

"It doesn't look injured," Cricket said. "Wouldn't it look injured after hitting those blades?"

"Yeah, kind of like running into a bus, I would think."

"That's really weird. I wish we could take it home and show Grandpa."

"No way! You're not picking that thing up."

Cricket stood up. "Okay, but let's see if there are any more."

Chapter Three

"Seven dead bats does seem like a lot," Grandpa McKay said, nodding. He was flipping through a field guide while the girls finished their lunch. "Especially for only one turbine."

"There are dozens of turbines on the hills out there," Shilo said.

Cricket frowned and nibbled on the crust of her sandwich. "That's a lot of dead bats."

"Did they look like any of these?" Grandpa McKay asked.

The girls studied pictures of different species of bats he had found. Cricket pointed to a gray-brown bat with a yellowish face. "Its face was kind of flattened, like that one's. And it had the same ears, with black around the edges."

"But its fur was different," Shilo said. "It looked silvery."

Grandpa McKay turned the page. "Like this?"

The fur on the bat's back was tinged with white, giving it a frosty appearance. The fur looked soft and thick.

Both girls nodded. "That's it," Cricket said. "With the yellow face."

"Look how big its teeth are, Cricket!" Shilo shuddered.

"That's a hoary bat. It's the largest bat in Canada," Grandpa McKay said.

"I wanted to bring one back to show you—" Cricket began.

"But you can catch rabies from bats, right?" Shilo interrupted.

"Rabies is pretty rare nowadays here in Alberta, but it's best not to touch any dead animal. It's strange you couldn't see any injuries. You're sure these bats ran into the turbine? Their echolocation should have helped them fly around the turbine, just like they fly around trees and houses."

"Their what?" Shilo asked.

Grandpa McKay propped his reading glasses on his head and looked at the girls. "Bats use echolocation to fly at night and catch moths and other insects. They make high-pitched sounds

BATS

that humans can't hear. When the sound waves bounce off an object, they can tell where it is and what it is and whether to eat it or fly around it."

"That's like dolphins." Tyler walked into the kitchen, carrying his fishing rod. "Did you find some more bats?"

Cricket nodded. "But they're dead. It looks like they ran into the turbine by mistake."

Tyler looked over Grandpa's shoulder at the photos. "Maybe the turbine was turning too fast, and echolocation didn't work."

"But how come there are no dead bats under the windmill at the dugout?" Shilo asked. "The turbines are huge compared to the windmill. It should be easier to avoid them, shouldn't it?"

"And where are the bats coming from?There aren't any caves around here," Tyler said. "It seems like there's more bats than usual."

Grandpa McKay nodded. "That's true. Some bats hibernate here in the winter but not hoary bats. They must have started their migration already, going south for the winter. That might be why it seems like there are more bats around."

"I still don't understand why they don't look injured," Shilo said.

"I think I know how we can figure it out." Cricket smiled. "I've got a plan."

Chapter Four

"Okay, I think we're ready." Cricket lifted her backpack onto the kitchen table and filled it with flashlights and snacks. Grandpa McKay handed her a small first-aid kit. "Are you guys coming? Tyler? Shilo? I want to get out there before the sun goes down."

"Did you remember the snacks?" Tyler asked.

Cricket rolled her eyes. Food was always a priority with Tyler. “Grandma packed us—Shilo! What are you doing?”

Shilo walked into the kitchen wearing an old white hockey helmet.

"It's perfect, don't you think?" Tyler grinned. "The bats can't fly into her hair, and she can't get lost. I put a glow-in-the-dark sticker on the back. We could see Shilo a mile away."

Cricket's mouth was open, but she didn't know whether to laugh or get mad at Tyler.

Grandpa McKay smiled and shook his head. "Bats don't purposely fly into your hair, Shilo. They're just chasing insects. If they swoop too close to you and get tangled, it probably scares them as much as it scares you."

"Terrifies, you mean," Shilo said.

"Yes, well, if you braid your hair and wear your ballcap, you should be fine."

"Are you sure?"

Grandpa McKay nodded. "Honestly."

She unsnapped the cage and lifted the helmet off her head. "Good, 'cause it's way too hot to wear that thing."

The three kids and Cooper reached the wind turbine just before the sun slipped behind the mountains far in the west. The wind had picked up speed and was blowing the tall grass almost flat to the ground. Once again Cooper sat down when they got close to the turbine.

"This is close enough for me too," Cricket said. The kids watched the blades of the turbine beat the air, spinning much more quickly than they had the day before. The steady hum was louder too, and the air made a *whoosh*ing sound as the blades spun.

Tyler was fascinated. "When it's spinning like that, the tips of the blades are going over two hundred miles an hour," he said to the girls. "It's the opposite of a fan. A fan uses energy to make wind, but a turbine uses wind to make energy. It's really cool."

Shilo was impressed. "Do you think it makes a lot of power?"

"Maybe two megawatts," Tyler said. "Enough to power seven hundred and fifty houses—about half of the town of Pincher Creek." He shrugged. "Or something like that. I looked it up on the Internet this afternoon."

Cricket made a face. Tyler loved researching stuff, even when he wasn't in school.

Cooper wagged his tail happily as the kids settled onto the grass beside him.

The sky gradually turned from pink to gray-blue to inky black.

Shilo pointed. "*Star light, star bright, first star I see tonight, I wish I may, I wish I might, have the wish I wish tonight.*"

"Cool," Tyler said, lying on his back in the grass. "But I thought we'd see lots of bats by now. Have you seen any?"

Cricket shook her head and lay down. "I haven't seen anything yet."

"Wow, the stars out here are amazing." Shilo pointed again. She didn't seem to be worried about the darkness as long as Cooper was snuggled beside her. "Look, there's the Big Dipper."

"Uh-huh. It's in the constellation Ursa Major, or the Great Bear," Tyler said. "And about twenty-five degrees to the east is Ursa Minor and Polaris."

Shilo turned and looked at Cricket. She shrugged.

"Where? How am I supposed to know how far twenty-five degrees is?" Shilo asked.

"Just hold out your fist, then stick out your baby finger and your thumb. That should measure about twenty-five degrees," Tyler said as he demonstrated with his right hand. "Put your baby finger on Ursa Major, and your thumb will point to Ursa Minor."

Shilo raised her hand. "Hey, I think it works! Polaris is really bright, right?"

The sky was completely clear, and all the constellations twinkled.

"What's that?" Shilo asked. "See the one that's moving? It's really bright, and it's not blinking."

"It's not a shooting star," Cricket said.

"Nope, I think it's the International Space Station. It orbits the earth a few times a day. Of course, there are lots of satellites too, and sometimes they look like shooting stars." Tyler sat up and dug into the backpack for a snack.

A low, mournful howl echoed over the hills. Cooper stood up and whined. His ears were flat against his head.

Shilo scrambled to her feet. "Was that a coyote or a wolf?"

"I dunno, but I think it's time to go." Cricket passed her a large flashlight that was more like a spotlight. It lit up the ground all around them.

"I haven't seen a single bat, have you?" Tyler asked. "Maybe they fly so high, we can't see them."

"Or maybe it's too windy for them." Cricket pulled the straps of the backpack over her shoulders as another howl echoed over the hills. "Let's get out of here!"

Chapter Five

The next day the girls walked out to the turbine after lunch. The wind had died down a bit but was still blowing enough to keep the blades spinning quickly. The long grass rippled with the gusts like waves on the ocean. The girls split up to walk around the base of the turbine, searching for bats.

"I haven't found a single one, not even the dead ones we saw yesterday," Cricket called to Shilo. "Have you?"

Shilo looked up. “Nope. Look, somebody’s coming.”

Cricket turned to see a white pickup truck driving up the gravel road. As it got closer she could see an energy-company logo on the door. When it stopped, a woman in blue coveralls got out.

“Hello there! What are you girls doing out here? You really shouldn’t play around the turbine.”

“Oh, we’re not playing,” Shilo said. “We’re looking for bats.”

The woman looked surprised.

“Not flying bats—dead ones,” Cricket explained. “We found a bunch on the ground yesterday morning and wanted to see if there would be more today.”

“Really?” The woman still looked surprised. “And are there any?”

Cricket shook her head. "We think they were hoary bats, but we can't figure out what killed them."

"And the ones we found yesterday are gone," Shilo said.

"Well, there are lots of scavengers around that might have taken them," the woman said. "But you haven't found any today?"

"We didn't see any bats at all last night. It was really windy, and the turbine was spinning like crazy," Cricket said.

The woman dug into her pocket and pulled out a business card. "Tell you what. Why don't you let me know if you find any more dead bats," she said. "My name's Grace Lee, and my email is right there on the card. It's my job to monitor these turbines."

Cricket nodded. "Thanks. I'm Cricket, and this is Shilo. This is my grandpa's farm."

"Nice to meet you girls. Cute dog." She nodded at Cooper, who was in his usual spot. He stood up and wagged his tail as they all turned to look at him.

"He's smart too. Remember, it's best not to get too close to the turbine." She climbed back into her truck and waved as she turned around toward the gate.

Cricket frowned. "She seemed surprised about the bats. We need to figure out what's killing them—and I really hope it's not the turbine."

Later that afternoon the girls sat on the porch, bored and worried. It was good that they didn't find any dead bats, but why didn't they? Was Tyler right—did the bats fly higher when it was windier? Was it because they could avoid the turbine easier when it was spinning faster? That didn't make sense.

"Do you girls need something to do?" Cricket's grandma held the back door open. "Why don't you come inside? I'm making cookies."

Shilo jumped up. "All right!"

As the girls walked into the kitchen, Grandma McKay pointed to the table. "There's a little project for you while the cookies are baking."

Cricket picked up the book and looked at Shilo. "Origami?"

Shilo shrugged. She picked up a sheet of paper from the stack on the table. It was square and very thin, almost like tissue paper. "Isn't that Japanese?"

"Yup, Japanese paper folding. Look, here's instructions on how to make a frog or a paper crane."

Shilo looked over Cricket's shoulder as she flipped through the book. "Hey, there's a bat!"

"It doesn't look too tricky," Cricket said.

The girls sat down and began following the instructions, step by step.

By the time Cricket's grandma put a plate of cookies on the table, they had made almost a dozen colorful paper bats.

Tyler appeared in the doorway. "Do I smell cookies?"

Cricket rolled her eyes, and Shilo giggled.

"Are you guys going into town with us?" Tyler asked. "Grandpa's going to register for the parade."

"Sure!" Shilo grabbed her hat, ready to go. "Thanks for the cookies, Mrs. McKay!"

Cricket looked out the truck window as they drove into town. She liked watching for wildlife and was usually the first one to spot a deer or coyote. Once she'd even seen a mother moose and calf strolling through a field. Today the wind turbines caught her eye. They marched across the hills in rows, like tall white soldiers.

Cricket frowned. The wind had died down completely. The summer heat had settled in, and there wasn't a cloud in the sky—so why were the blades of the turbines still spinning?

"Grandpa, do you think those turbines are making any power? They're turning so slowly."

"I really don't know, Cricket. You'll have to ask the power company about that."

She looked at Tyler, and he shrugged. "I don't know either," he said.

"I would think they'd just stop if there was no wind," Shilo said, "but maybe someone has to turn them off."

Cricket nodded. "So why don't they?"

Chapter Six

The next afternoon the girls and Cooper headed out to the back pasture again. Tyler stayed behind to help Grandpa polish his truck. Grandpa planned to drive a real antique in the parade on Saturday—the truck *his* grandpa had driven more than ninety years earlier. It was red, with the farm brand, **McK**, in faded yellow paint on the doors.

"It looks like the turbine lady is here again," Shilo said. The energy-company pickup truck was parked near the base of the turbine, and Ms. Lee was using the radio.

"And what is all that?" Cricket was looking at a stack of enormous white pipes next to the fence. "Those weren't here yesterday."

"They look like the bases for the wind turbines," Shilo said. "You don't think they're planning on building more of them here, do you?"

Ms. Lee waved to the girls as she got out of the truck. "Let's go ask," Cricket said.

As they walked over to the truck, Cricket almost missed the small brown lump lying in the grass. Then Shilo found another—and another.

"It happened again!" Cricket said, using her shoe to roll the bat over. "It's just like the other ones."

"What did you find, girls? What's just like the others?" Ms. Lee approached them with a look of concern on her face.

Cricket stood up. "There are more dead bats," she said.

"Lots of them," Shilo added. "At least five right here."

Ms. Lee frowned and crouched down to study the tiny bat. She took a pen out of a pocket of her coveralls and spread out its wings. "Do they all look like this?" she asked.

The girls nodded.

"The turbines were turning really slowly last night," Cricket said. "Do they make any power when they turn so slowly?"

"Not much, but when the wind picks up, they can start generating more power right away, without waiting for me to turn them on. I'm sure you girls know how quickly the weather can change here in southern Alberta."

"Well, it seems like the bats run into them when they're barely turning but not when they're spinning fast," Shilo said.

Ms. Lee looked up at the blades of the turbine. They had picked up speed as the wind started to blow harder. "We didn't find any dead bats earlier in the summer," she said.

"My grandpa says they are migrating right now. They're flying through here on their way to Arizona and Mexico," Cricket said.

Ms. Lee put the pen back in her pocket. "Thanks for showing me this, girls. I've got to get back to work now." She turned and started to walk back to her truck.

"Wait! What are all those for? Are you building more turbines here?" Cricket pointed to the huge stack of metal tubes.

"Yes, six more Vestas V80s. Construction starts next week."

The girls watched Ms. Lee turn her truck around and drive away. They looked at each other in dismay.

"Why would they do that, right in the middle of the migration?" Cricket said.

"I bet they just don't know." Shilo pulled her hat down tight. The wind was gusting stronger, and the turbines had really picked up speed.

Cooper gave a high-pitched yip. He was standing up, watching the girls closely. He wagged his tail as they walked toward him, then squeezed in between them.

"What's up with him?" Shilo asked. "Why isn't he chasing ground squirrels?"

Cricket looked around. There were no ground squirrels. No furry heads popped out of burrows. No little black eyes watched them as they walked through the grass. Then she looked up.

"Uh-oh." Huge dark rain clouds rolled toward them. The clouds blocked out the sun. The air felt cooler as it whipped through the grass.

Shilo gasped. "Is it a tornado?"

"No," Cricket said. "It just looks like a really bad rainstorm. Maybe even hail."

They started to jog. Giant drops of rain began to fall.

"We aren't going to make it back to the house!"

Cricket looked around. "Come on! The old hay shed is right over there."

Chapter Seven

The girls sprinted through the rain. They had almost reached the hay shed when the rain turned to chunks of ice. The hail pummeled them, bouncing off their shoulders and heads.

"Ouch!" Shilo tried to cover her head with her arms as she ran. Cooper streaked ahead to the shed.

Cricket pulled open the wooden door. It was dark and musty inside the shed.

She stepped in, then turned around. Shilo was frozen in the doorway.

"Come on, Shilo!" Cricket yelled. Hailstones pounded on the roof of the shed. The roar got louder. The hail dropped like a curtain of ice.

Shilo yelped and jumped inside.

Cricket closed the door partway to block the wind. She shook her hair, and bits of ice went flying into the darkness. She wiped her face with her sleeve.

Shilo knelt down to brush bits of ice from Cooper's fur. She looked up at Cricket and her eyes widened. Her mouth dropped open.

"What?" Cricket's voice was drowned out by the noise of the hail on the shed roof. Shilo pointed over her shoulder.

Cricket looked up. Hundreds of eyes looked back at her. She gasped and dropped to the floor beside Shilo and Cooper.

Bats! Hundreds of bats hung from the rafters of the shed. They were all wide-awake, watching the girls and shifting restlessly. But none of them flew away. None of them attacked.

Shilo slowly reached out to grab Cricket's hand. She was trembling. It was hard not to panic, stuck in the dark with hundreds of bats!

Cricket squeezed her hand and pulled her over to the wall. The girls sat there, listening to the storm. Cooper sat next to Shilo and leaned against her, panting.

Cricket watched the bats watching her. *They're so small,* she thought, *and brown.* She studied them more closely. *Where was the yellow marking? Why were these bats completely brown?*

She leaned close to Shilo. "These are different bats!" she whispered.

"What?" Shilo mouthed.

Cricket pointed, but Shilo shook her head and frowned. It was impossible to talk while the storm roared outside.

After a few minutes the wind seemed to die down. The hail was falling less sharply on the roof. It sounded more like steady rain.

Cricket peeked out the door. "It's almost over," she said.

Shilo nodded. She didn't take her eyes off the bats, watching for any sign of attack.

"Hey! I see some headlights!" Cricket opened the door wide. "It's Grandpa!"

Shilo inched her way along the wall and out the door. The rain was slowing, and the sky was getting brighter.

"How did you find us, Grandpa?" Cricket asked as they climbed into the truck beside him. Cooper jumped into the backseat.

"I figured you girls would take shelter. It's a good thing I haven't torn down that old hay shed yet."

"You can't tear it down, Grandpa! The bats will have nowhere to go."

Shilo shuddered. "There's hundreds of them in there."

Grandpa McKay looked at them in surprise. "Really?"

"But they aren't the same as the ones we found by the turbines," Cricket said. "They're much smaller and don't look frosted. They're completely brown."

"That makes sense. Hoary bats roost in trees, not buildings," Grandpa McKay said as he turned the truck around and headed for home. "You must have found a colony of little brown bats. They've probably been living in the shed all summer."

"But it's dark now," Cricket said. "Why haven't they left the shed?"

"No bats like to fly in the wind, and they definitely won't fly in a storm like this."

"Do you think that's why we didn't find any dead bats under the turbine yesterday? Because it was too windy for them?" Cricket asked.

Her grandpa nodded. "Most likely."

"So if it's really windy, the turbines make lots of power—"

"But that's okay, because there's no bats," Shilo added.

"And when it's not windy enough to make much power, it's perfect conditions for the bats to migrate—"

“So the power company should just turn the turbines off!”

“We need to let Ms. Lee know! Maybe she can turn the turbines off during the migration,” Cricket said.

Chapter Eight

Before they went to bed that night, Cricket found Ms. Lee's business card in her backpack and wrote her an email.

"Be sure to tell her our idea about turning off the turbines just while the bats are migrating," Shilo said as she peered over Cricket's shoulder.

"You could add that the efficiency of the turbines drops a lot as the wind slows," Tyler added. "In fact, if the wind slows to half the optimum speed, the turbine's efficiency is reduced by a factor of eight. It makes almost no power at such a slow speed."

The girls looked at him, then looked at each other.

"Um, Ms. Lee monitors the turbines," Cricket said. "I'm sure she knows all that technical stuff."

"Do you think she knows the hoary bats' migration could last a couple of weeks?"

"That's good. I'll include that."

Cricket finished typing, made a silent wish and sent the email.

The next morning there was no reply from Ms. Lee.

"Don't let that get you down, girls," Grandma McKay said as they sat down for breakfast.

"I expect the power company gets lots of emails with questions and petitions from farmers and ranchers about those turbines." Grandpa McKay helped himself to a warm blueberry muffin.

"Maybe that's what we need—a petition to stop the turbines," Shilo said.

Cricket thought about that as she chewed on a piece of bacon. "That would take too long," she said.

"Be patient, girls." Grandma McKay winked at Cricket. "Sometimes people can surprise you."

Patience was going to be difficult. Cricket was worried about the bat migration *right now*.

Grandpa McKay dusted muffin crumbs off his shirt and went out to finish polishing the truck while the girls helped Grandma clean up. Shilo was curious—and excited—about the parade, asking all kinds of questions while she dried the dishes. But Cricket dried the same plate three times, distracted by the bat problem. What could they do to help? Maybe they could tell more people about the bats. Not with a petition. But how?

"So what do you think, Cricket?"

"What? About what?"

Shilo rolled her eyes. "Earth to Cricket! We were talking about the parade, of course."

The parade! Cricket's mind started jumping with ideas. Maybe they could do something in the parade!

"Uh-oh," Shilo said. "I think she's got an idea."

The girls spent the rest of the day making plans for the parade. They gathered poster paper, markers, black tape and garbage bags. Grandpa agreed to let one of them ride in the back of the truck during the parade, and even Tyler got excited when he heard their plan.

"I've got a great idea! Can I build something for the back of the truck?" he asked.

"Sure, but—" Cricket said.

Tyler was already heading out the door. "It'll be a surprise," he called over his shoulder. "You're going to love it!"

Shilo looked at Cricket and laughed. "He didn't even hear about his costume! Do you think he'll do it?"

"If we have enough cookies, Tyler will do anything."

Chapter Nine

Early the next morning Grandma McKay drove the kids into town to meet Grandpa. Shilo yawned for the sixth time.

"How late did you girls work last night?" Grandma McKay asked.

Cricket settled an enormous stuffed garbage bag on her lap. "Um, not too late."

"Just long enough to make two hun—"

Cricket poked Shilo with her elbow. "Are you going to watch the parade, Grandma?"

Grandma McKay nodded and glanced at Tyler. "Cookies for breakfast, Tyler? What have the girls talked you into?"

He made a face and brushed crumbs off his shirt. "It sounded like a better idea last night," he said.

The park at the far end of Main Street was colorful and crowded as floats and people gathered before the start of the parade. Parade officials walked around with clipboards, trying to organize the chaos. The high-school marching band was warming up over by the railway tracks. The 4-H-club kids were wiping the last bit of dirt from their calves and

braiding their horses' manes. An antique tractor rattled at the curb, and the mayor perched on the back of a convertible, ready to lead the parade.

"Hey, there's Will!" Tyler waved to his best friend from Waterton. He was driving a four-wheeled bike with a big sign advertising his dad's business, Pat's Garage. A giant bucket of candy sat on the seat beside him. "We should give out candy too—or maybe spray people with water guns."

"We have something even better," Shilo said.

Cricket carefully set the garbage bag into the back of the truck. "Something nobody's ever seen before—at least, not at a parade." She reached into the truck for a roll of black tape and two pieces of plastic she had cut from black garbage bags.

It all matched Tyler's black shirt and shorts. "Are you ready?"

"I don't think you paid me with enough cookies," he grumbled as Cricket put the finishing touches on his costume. When she was done, he climbed up into the back of the truck, where Grandpa had stacked hay bales for him to lean on. He would be able to stand up safely while the truck was moving.

"Just think of all the lives you'll save," Shilo said as she tossed him a pair of black gloves and a knitted black cap.

Grandpa McKay joined the girls and grinned up at Tyler. "Everybody ready? Tyler, do you need help attaching the pinwheel?"

"The what?" Cricket looked at Tyler in surprise.

"It's a turbine, Grandpa." Tyler lifted a tall wooden structure from the back of the truck. The whirligig from the farm's old windmill was nailed at the top, and the entire thing was painted white. "It's not perfect, but—"

"It's great!" the girls exclaimed.

"Well, good, 'cause it was pretty tricky climbing up to get this thing off the windmill." Tyler strapped the structure to the truck with a bungee cord.

"And it will be just as tricky putting it back," Grandpa said. "Don't forget these, girls." He reached into the truck for two large signs.

"The one with the bat on it is mine," Shilo said reaching for the bright yellow sign that read *Bats Migrate Here!*

Grandpa handed Cricket the second sign. "I like your slogan. No Wind—No

Spin should get people thinking." He turned and climbed into the truck as the mayor's convertible started to rumble.

The parade organizer's voice squawked over a loudspeaker. "It's showtime!"

A loud cheer went up, and the parade began to surge forward.

Chapter Ten

"Quick, Tyler, pass us some bats!"

Tyler opened the garbage bag and carefully passed a handful of colorful origami bats to the girls. "I still think candy would be better," he said. He rolled down his ski mask so all that showed were his eyes and mouth. He pulled on the black gloves. "I look like I'm ready for a blizzard, but that's okay—this way no one will recognize me."

Grandpa McKay drove into position behind the marching band and began to creep along the parade route. Little kids sat on the curb, chattering with excitement. Grandparents sat in lawn chairs on the sidewalk, and older kids and adults stood behind them. Police cruisers blocked the side streets, and Cricket spotted her grandmother sitting with her friends in lawn chairs in front of the café.

"It's kind of loud here," Shilo said as the band started to play.

"Yeah, but I'd rather follow the band than a bunch of horses," Cricket said. "At least we don't have to jump over horse poop."

Shilo laughed. She spotted a group of little kids on the curb. "Do you guys like bats?" she called.

The kids stared at her. "Bats? They're creepy."

"How about these bats?" Shilo handed each of them an origami bat and showed them how to squeeze the body to make the wings flap.

"Cool!"

"Hey, look! There's a giant bat!" One of the kids pointed to Grandpa McKay's truck. Tyler stretched his arms out and pretended to swoop. The black plastic opened up under his arms like bat wings. The windmill was spinning beside him. Cricket, Shilo and Tyler had the crowd's full attention.

A little girl in pink shorts ran up to Cricket. "Can I have a bat too, please?"

"What does No Wind—No Spin mean?" someone asked.

BATS
MIGRATE
HERE
NO
WIND
NO
SPIN!

"Do you mean the turbines?" another person asked.

Cricket nodded. She looked over and saw Shilo talking to a group of people and pointing at Tyler, who swooped and flapped in the back of the truck. They had people's attention—but would that be enough?

As they neared the end of the parade route, Cricket and Shilo dug out the last few handfuls of origami bats. A man carrying a large camera approached the truck and walked alongside, talking to Grandpa McKay. He wore a badge that said *Pincher Creek Echo*.

"He's from the newspaper, Cricket," Shilo said. "You should go talk to him."

Cricket's eyes widened, and her heart thumped. This was her chance to tell even more people about the bat migration. Grandpa waved her over.

"Cricket, this is Mr. Nelson. He's got some questions about your signs, and I thought you could explain the problem better than I could," he said, then winked. "I think he wants a few pictures of Tyler too."

The reporter had no idea that thousands of bats were migrating through Pincher Creek. He nodded and took notes as Cricket explained where the bats were going and how dangerous the wind turbines were. He frowned when she told him about the dead bats they had found.

"So Cricket, what do you think should be done about this?" he asked.

"We need the power, but we need the bats too," Cricket said. "If the power company stopped the turbines on the nights when there is no wind, the bats could pass through more safely. It's only for a few weeks, while they're migrating."

Mr. Nelson nodded.

"But we don't know how to get their attention. We're hoping some of these people will help."

"I'll get the power company's side of the story, and we'll see what they think of your idea. It sounds pretty simple." He handed Cricket a business card. "You can check out photos of the parade—they're already online." Mr. Nelson tapped his phone, and the newspaper website popped up. He scrolled down to a photo of Tyler, midswoop. The caption underneath read *"Bat-boy" Tyler McKay shows that wind turbines and bats don't mix*.

Cricket grinned. Tyler was right—they hadn't paid him nearly enough cookies.

Chapter Eleven

Questions about the bats didn't stop when the parade ended. Everywhere they went that afternoon, the kids were asked about bats. The owner of the corner store quizzed them as he scooped their ice cream. In the bookstore and at the diner, people wanted to talk about bats. Even a policeman pulled over to the curb to ask questions. It was funny to hear Shilo explain that bats don't attack people.

"I'm tired of talking," Cricket said as she settled into the truck.

"It's amazing how many people think bats are dangerous," Shilo said, shaking her head.

"Yeah, or how many people have never even seen a bat."

"It's even more amazing how many people recognized me in that crazy bat costume," Tyler said.

Cricket and Shilo looked at each other and laughed. "It's not really *that* amazing. Grandma, can I borrow your phone?"

Tyler groaned when he saw the photo. He scrolled down. "Hey, Cricket, did you see this?"

The newspaper had posted pictures of real bats and the wind turbines. Mr. Nelson had written an article about the girls and their concern about the danger to the bats during their migration.

"There's a picture of Ms. Lee," Shilo said. "Did you know she's an engineer? She says the power company is going to do a study of the wind turbines and bat mortality."

Cricket frowned. A study could take months or years. The migration was happening right now, and the bats needed help right away.

When they got home Tyler checked the newspaper's website again. More than three hundred people had looked at the article.

"Lots of people are making comments. They want the power company to turn the turbines off so the bats can migrate safely," Tyler said.

Shilo looked over his shoulder. "Hey, look at this one, Cricket. Someone wants our instructions for making origami bats."

"And Ms. Lee answered your email! She says she will take your suggestion into consideration, whatever that means."

"It means you got them thinking," Grandpa McKay said. "I would say your plan was a success."

Tyler and Shilo nodded, but Cricket sighed and looked out the kitchen window. Wispy clouds slipped across the sky. Sunflowers nodded their heads in the breeze. By the time the sun went down, the evening would be clear and still—a perfect night for migrating bats.

After dinner Cricket and Shilo tossed their flashlights into a backpack and headed out the back door. Cooper yipped and spun in circles, then took off into the field.

Shilo laughed. "How does he know where we're going?"

"Probably the same way I do," Tyler said as he walked around the corner of the garage. "Can I come with you? I brought snacks."

Cricket rolled her eyes and Shilo laughed.

"Sure," Shilo said. "You can help scare away the coyotes."

As they crossed the field Cooper zigzagged, looking for ground squirrels. The sky was deepening to a dark blue, but the full moon was rising quickly. The clumps of trees near the hay shed were ink-black shadows. Not a leaf was moving. Cricket was worried.

If our plan had really been a success, she thought, the power company would have agreed to stop the turbines right away. Suddenly a dark cloud erupted from under the eaves of the shed and flew up into the night.

Shilo squeaked. "Did you see that? Did you see all those bats?"

"That was so cool!" Tyler said. "There must have been hundreds of them."

Cricket nodded. She had a knot in the pit of her stomach.

"Don't worry, Cricket," Tyler said. "Those bats will be safe. Grandpa told me little brown bats don't fly high enough to be killed by the turbines. They're hunting bugs that are closer to the ground."

"That must be why we didn't find any of them under the turbines," Cricket said as they followed Cooper around the trees. "It's just the hoary bats that are being killed."

"Not tonight!" Shilo said. She pointed at the turbine. It stood like a ghost in the night sky, tall and white and...completely still! The blades of the turbine weren't turning.

The kids cheered.

"They did it! They stopped the turbines!"

"*We* did it!"

All the turbines that marched across the hills beyond the farm stood perfectly still. Cricket smiled and high-fived Shilo and Tyler. The ball of worry in her stomach melted away. The kids hurried to the spot where they had stargazed a few nights earlier, tossed their backpacks and laid down on the grass.

Cooper collapsed beside Cricket and rested his chin on her leg.

"Do you need a flashlight, Shilo?" Cricket asked.

"Not tonight. The moon's so bright, I almost need sunglasses."

"There! I see one!" Tyler pointed directly overheard. "And another one!"

Cricket craned her neck, searching the sky. "Where? I don't see anything."

"You have to look straight up," Tyler said.

And then she saw them, small black creatures darting across the sky, all heading in the same direction. She couldn't hear the bats making any noise, but Cooper's ears twitched back and forth. Cricket started counting them, then gave up. There were just too many bats!

"Good thing Ms. Lee stopped the turbines tonight," Shilo said. "Do you think she'll do it again?"

"A lot of people like our idea," Cricket said. "And when the power company does their study, they'll find out we were right."

"We could write letters and start a petition too, like we did for the salamanders," Shilo said.

Cricket smiled as she watched the bats overhead, on their way to Mexico or Guatemala, or whatever warm country they visited for the winter. By next year their migration through southern Alberta would be safer.

Epilogue

Not a lot is known about bat migration, but bats appear to fly along the same windy corridors that are the best locations for wind farms. Some bats are killed when they run into the blades of the turbine, but more are killed when they fly through the zone of low pressure created by the spinning blades. The low pressure causes the air in their lungs to expand so rapidly that internal organs are damaged. Scientists don't know why bats fly close to wind turbines. It could be because their echolocation can detect solid objects but not low-pressure zones, or perhaps because the turbines are four times taller than windmills were and are now in the bats' flyway. Some scientists even suggest that bats are attracted to the turbines because they appear to be large trees.

In 2005 scientists at Summerview wind farm near Pincher Creek, Alberta, discovered a way to save the lives of some migrating bats. As a test, the power company TransAlta stopped the turbines when wind was low in the fall, during the migratory season. Scientists found 50 percent fewer dead bats near the base of those turbines.

Why should we spend so much time and money studying an animal many people fear? Bats are the only flying mammal and—most important—the only nocturnal flying insectivore, which means bats are the only insect-eating mammals that fly at night. One bat can eat three thousand insects a night! Bats help to control agricultural pests naturally by eating the insects that could destroy farm crops. Without bats, we might rely more on chemicals that are harmful to the environment and the animals and people living there. Without bats, the ecological balance would be upset, and the insect population could explode. We may not see bats very often, but we would quickly notice if they were gone.

Pamela McDowell's first career was in education, teaching junior high and high school. She has written more than forty nonfiction books for children. Pamela grew up in Alberta and enjoys writing about the diverse animals and habitats of her home province. Pamela lives in Calgary, Alberta, with her husband, two kids and an Australian shepherd. For more information, visit www.pamelamcdowell.ca.

Also by Pamela McDowell

Ages 7–9 • $6.95
9781459802834 PB
9781459802841 (pdf)
9781459802858 (epub)

Ages 7–9 • $6.95
9781459811232 PB
9781459811249 (pdf)
9781459811256 (epub)